Bob the Builder™

New Boots for Bob!

adapted by Kiki Thorpe

based on a book by Diane Redmond

Ready-to-Read

Simon Spotlight

New York   London   Toronto   Sydney   Singapore

Based upon the television series *Bob the Builder*™
created by HIT Entertainment PLC and Keith Chapman,
as seen on Nick Jr.® Photos by HOT Animation.

SIMON SPOTLIGHT
An imprint of Simon & Schuster Children's Publishing Division
1230 Avenue of the Americas, New York, New York 10020
© 2003 HIT Entertainment PLC and Keith Chapman.
Manufactured in the United States of America
First Edition
2 4 6 8 10 9 7 5 3 1

Library of Congress Cataloging-in-Publication Data
Thorpe, Kiki.
New boots for Bob! / adapted by Kiki Thorpe
p. cm.—(Bob the builder. Ready-to-read ; 5)
Summary: Bob has a new pair of boots that make a funny squeaking sound
when he walks.
ISBN 0-689-85277-0
[1. Boots—Fiction.] I. Title. II. Bob the builder. Preschool ready- to- read ; 5.
PZ7.T3974 Ne 2003
[E]—dc21
2002004840

Look at Bob!

Bob has something new.

Bob has new boots!

Bob walks this way.

Squeak, squeak, squeak.

Bob walks that way.

Squeak, squeak, squeak.

What is that sound?

It is the new boots!

The new boots go
squeak, squeak, squeak.

Bob and Lofty
go to work.

The new boots go

Squeak, Squeak, Squeak.

Here are three mice.

The mice hear

squeak, squeak, squeak.

What is that sound?

It is the new boots!

Squeak, squeak, squeak.

The mice like the boots.

Lofty does not like mice.
Lofty runs away.

Bob runs after Lofty.

Squeak, Squeak, Squeak.

Lofty is scared.

Here comes Spud.

Spud has a bun.

Squeak, squeak, squeak.
The mice want Spud's
bun.

The mice run after Spud.
Run, Spud, run!

Lofty is happy.
The mice are gone!

Bob is happy.
He has new boots!